Beau Monde Estates

KC SAVAGE

Lyla J
CREATIONS

Edited by Writing Evolution

Cover designed by Eve Graphic Design

Proofread by Andrea Barreiro

Printed by Amazon Inc., in the United States of America.

First printing, 2025

Lyla D Creations LLC

Florida

❀ Formatted with Vellum

Disclaimer

These stories contain
Adultery
Lying
DV/abuse
Mentions of miscarriage and infertility
Sexually explicit scenes,
Strong language.

Please read at your own risk.

Blurb

Behind the gates of the Beau Monde Estates.

Where the illusion of perfection permeates everywhere.

They want for nothing with designer clothes, fancy vehicles, enormous homes.

Roxi, Layne, Khloe, and Dottie's precarious lives play out in these four stories, where they find themselves in need of
Elio, an air-conditioning repairman,
Beckett, a pool guy,
Diego, an electrician,
and Ace, a handyman.

Can these blue-collar men fulfill the disenchanted desires of the wealthy women of the Beau Monde Estates?

Blown
Drenched

Plugged
Screwed

Þlown

Roxi

Our eyes meet as I take the iPad from Elio, the AC repairman. The intense desire coming from his gaze fills me with sensual impulses. I breathe in his clean, fresh scent as he stands too close to me. I bite my lip, when he smiles sinfully. Breaking his stare, I look down and read, then sign the iPad giving him permission to fix the air-conditioning unit. It's fucking August in Florida.

Beads of sweat form on my forehead. My hair sticks to my neck. My husband and I were up sweating all night as the ceiling fan didn't help cool us. It only moved the hot air around us.

A slight nudge of his hip causes me to tilt my head. The heat behind his brown eyes makes my breath hitch. My pussy clench.

I haven't been fucked in over five years. My sex drive seemed nonexistent, then Elio showed up. Suddenly, my body heats up with a desire for him to take me however he wants to. I imagine how good Elio would make me feel. How his large hands would feel kneading my breasts. His mouth sucking my nipples. How his full lips would feel against mine. I want him! God, I need to be fucked, and soon. I swallow hard to quelch my instant thirst for him.

"All signed. Now please, Elio, fix that damn unit and fast."

His soft hand covers mine as he takes the iPad from me. His gaze smolders with lust, causing me to bite back a moan. My legs quiver. My heart pounds fiercely. My nipples betray me, pebbling under my white tank top. I cross my arms to cover the evidence of my attraction to this hulk of a man.

A mischievous smile tugs on his full lips; I want them on me so fucking bad. I turn away to prevent something from happening that I won't be able to come back from. He grabs my arm, spinning me to face him. Holding my desperate gaze, he caresses my arm.

"Yes, Miss Roxi. Anything for you. Anything at all." He trails his fingers all the way down my forearm.

Millions of sparks ignite inside my body. My clit aches for attention. I open my mouth to speak, but words escape me as I watch Elio lick his lips. I nod as my eyes follow his tongue trail all the way around his mouth. It's soft. I know it, and fuck! How I want it on me. In me. All over me.

"Mmm," he purrs, sending more sensual waves through me, leaving my hunger for him purring between my legs.

Ducking his head, he turns and heads into the garage to work.

"Roxi!" Reese bellows.

"Coming, dear," I call out and rush up the stairs to my husband.

"Is the air conditioner going to be fixed today?"

"I don't know," I say while thinking of Elio hard at work downstairs.

"Let me know, because if it's not, I'm staying at the office tonight. It's too fucking hot to sleep here."

"Yes, dear. I'll call you when Elio lets me know."

"Fine." Reese grabs his phone, then goes into the bathroom.

He and several friends are partners at Defense Dynasty, a high-priced defense law firm in South Beach, Florida. We married thirty years ago. After I miscarried our baby boy, Reese changed. I was thirty-nine at the time, so we knew it was a slim chance I'd carry to term, but it still hit us both hard with immense grief. Where I tried to find comfort in my husband's arms though, Reese sought distance. I tried to talk to him. Tried to get him to go to counseling. He refused. Said everything was fine. We'd try again. And we did, but not with me.

We hired a surrogate and tried several times with IVF. Each time it failed, Reese blamed me. He said my eggs were too old even though we'd frozen them shortly after getting married. We'd known we'd wanted to wait to have a family. We talked about it a lot. He promised once he was finished with law school and was hired at one of the local law firms he'd have more time to be present and be the best father to our kids.

Reese was right about one thing; law school and interning for a law firm in the city took up almost all of his time. He was hardly ever home and I didn't want to raise a family alone. The last IVF failure happened five years ago; he's never touched me since.

"Miss Roxi," Elio calls out.

My heart rate speeds up, and heat rushes through me as I make my way into the kitchen.

"Yes, Elio." I lean against the counter, wiping my hand over my damp neck.

"Miss Roxi, I have good news and bad news." His gaze catches mine.

The heat between my legs is hotter than this house without air conditioning, but I push that from my mind as I say, "Bad news first, please."

"I have to get a part for your air conditioner."

"And the good news?"

"I'll be back tomorrow to fix it." He smiles wide and sinfully.

Elio

"Okay, Elio. I hope you can get it fixed. What time will you be back tomorrow?" Roxi asks as she gets a bottle of water from the refrigerator. "Want one?"

"Yes, thank you. I'll be here first thing around nine." I purposely cover her hand with mine as I take the bottle from her.

Her blue eyes, full of desire, meet mine. She bites her lip, then takes a sip from the bottle.

My cock twitches as I wish it were her lips on my dick, sucking me dry. But she's married to Reese Remington. The hotshot lawyer from Defense Dynasty with a shitty reputation of being the ruthless asshole in the South.

From what I've read, he represents the fucking greedy companies buying up all the foreclosed homes in South Florida. Those monsters only want money. They don't care if the buildings need basic repairs. When they're taken to court, most hire Reese Remington and get off scot-free. It's disgusting. My blood boils at the thought of my sweet Roxi being married to him. She deserves better. A better, honest working man. I doubt she knows who his clients are and how they treat regular everyday people.

I wish I could tell her who she's married to. How awful Reese Remington truly is, but that's not my place. He can't treat her like she deserves. He doesn't treat anyone that way, unless they have deep pockets, and take care of him.

I want to give her the honest life she deserves. I can't give her what she has now with this mansion of a house or the Porsche SUV parked in the garage. I can give her love, kindness, honesty and loyalty.

But for now, I'm indulging in this moment of simply being with her. If I get the chance, I'll give her all of me. I'll treat her with love and respect, then I'll rock her world.

"Roxi!" Mr. Remington yells as he enters the kitchen.

I step away from her.

"Yes, dear?" Roxi says calmly.

He ignores her and speaks to me. "Man, will you fix this fucking air-conditioning unit already?"

"Reese, don't talk like that," Roxi tells him. She glances at me, her eyes sad with guilt.

"I'm sorry, Mr. Remington. Not today. I'll be back tomorrow to fix it," I say confidently, although I don't know that for sure. The longer it takes to fix the air conditioner, the more I get to see Roxi.

Mr. Remington huffs out a breath and slams the countertop with his hand. "Fuck!" He turns toward Roxi and says, "I'll stay at the office tonight. You can do whatever you want, Roxi. But I'm not staying in this heat." He grabs his briefcase from the table, kisses her quickly on the cheek, then leaves.

Standing with her arms crossed under her perfect breasts, she sighs. Her head falls to her chest as she wipes the back of her neck with a hand towel.

When she looks at me, she smiles sadly. "I'm sorry, Elio.

Reese is frustrated. He's super busy and… yeah, I don't know anymore." Her smile fades. Her blue eyes fill with tears.

I want to take her into my arms and make her life happy. She's so gorgeous. She's so sweet. She deserves a better man. One who treasures her for her.

I shouldn't think this, but now that I'm alone with her, I have the opportunity to convince her to sleep with me; if only just once.

She clears her throat, grabbing my attention. "Okay, Elio. I guess I'll see you then." Fire replaces the tears that were in her eyes just a moment ago. A determined grin fills her face. She drags her hands through her hair, gathering the long blonde strands up into a messy bun. She takes a clip lying on the counter, and places it on her head.

She wipes the sweat off her neck again, then tosses the wet towel into the sink.

I hand her a dry one from my back pocket.

"Thank you, Elio," she says, reaching for the towel.

"You're welcome. What else can I do for you, Miss Roxi?" I ask, stepping closer to her.

Her head dips. Electric silence fills the space between us. She tilts her head. Her blue eyes meet mine. Her pink lips curve into a sexy smile. She averts her gaze as she hands the towel back to me.

I grasp her hand, gently pulling her to me. Standing so close, I breathe in her sweet and salty scent. I lean close to kiss her full lips, but she turns her head, and I kiss her soft cheek.

She presses her free hand on my chest, keeping us from embracing. She bites her lower lip, trying to hide a sweet smile as she steps further back from me.

My dark shorts hide my hard cock. I'd give anything to fuck her. Sweep her from her feet and fireman carry her to the dining room. I'd bend her over the enormous dining table and shove my dick into her sweet pussy.

My phone pings, bringing me back to reality. Glancing at it, I see my boss's text about the next appointment. Fuck. I need to go, but I don't want to.

"Elio," Roxi says, getting my attention. "Is everything okay?"

"Oh, yes, Miss Roxi. My boss texted me about the next job." I shake my head. "I need to go now. See you tomorrow morning."

"Yes. See you then." Roxi walks with me to the front door. She touches my bicep. Smiling up at me, she says, "Thank you for trying to fix the air-conditioning unit today."

"You're welcome. Sorry I didn't. But I get to come back and see you now." I wink and reach to touch her cheek. She presses her face against my palm, and I'm fighting the urge to leave. I lean closer to her, wanting to kiss her lips this time.

She pushes me back, bowing and shaking her head slowly. "I..." She steps back further and takes hold of the door. "I think you should send someone else to fix the AC tomorrow. Have a nice day, Elio." She shifts her eyes from mine.

Fuck! I was too aggressive when I tried to kiss her again. Slumping my shoulders, I nod and turn to walk to my work truck.

Once I'm out of sight of the Remington house, I pull over and text Roxi.

Me: I'm sorry if I over-stepped, Miss Roxi. How can I make it up to you? I'll do anything for you.

Roxi

I stare at his text message from yesterday. His apology seems sincere, and I reacted in haste when I told him to send another repairman. I know if he comes back here, I won't be able to control myself.

I wonder if he really means for me to call or text him for anything. What's anything? Coffee? Lunch? Dinner? Sex? God, how I wish.

The new air-conditioning guy comes and replaces the unit within four hours. I wait a few hours before texting Reese.

> Me: The AC is working. We got a new unit.
> How about a nice dinner?

I stare at my phone, waiting for my husband to respond. He's read it, but as usual, he makes me wait. After a half hour, his text tone sounds.

> Reese: It's about fucking time. I have a
> dinner meeting tonight, can't miss it. I'll just
> stay at the office again.

> Me: The house will be back to a normal cool temperature by the time your dinner meeting will be over. Please come home tonight, Reese. Please.

Another few minutes pass before he responds.

> Reese: The meeting is right by the office. I'll see you tomorrow night.

It's been a day and a half since I saw Reese. There's no, 'I love you, Roxi.' No, 'sorry honey.' No, 'I miss you, baby.' In any of his messages. What the fuck am I doing still in this marriage? Is he cheating on me? Is he bored with me? Maybe yes on both counts…

I fall into one of the breakfast nook chairs and stare at my phone. I pan back through the messages with Reese. My heart slows as I realize there's no love in any of the texts. I don't hate Reese. I hate what our marriage has become. To the outside world, we have it all. Nice house. Nice vehicles. Money. Status within our circle of friends. But that's not everything. Love is everything, and that's what's missing.

A pinch like an arrow pierces me, and I gasp, pressing my fist against my chest. I blink quickly to keep the tears that are welling in my eyes from falling.

I don't want to cheat on my husband. Thirty years of marriage is too much to walk away from just because some young man was nice to me.

I decide to make Reese's favorite dessert, coconut cake. It's definitely not my favorite at all. I hate coconut, and he knows that. I'll make him a cake and take it into the office as a surprise for after his dinner meeting. Maybe this impromptu act of kindness will soften his heart, and he'll take the time to actually see me again. I'm going to try to save our fledgling marriage one last time.

Baking cakes and cookies was my favorite thing to do for Reese when we first married. He has the biggest sweet-tooth. I used to bake for him every week. Then after the miscarriage, I lost all interest in it.

Once the cake has cooled enough for me to place it in the cake carrier, I head out to my SUV, and place it on the floorboard of the front passenger seat.

When I get to Reese's office building, I check for his SUV to be sure he's back from his dinner meetings. I want to surprise him with the coconut cake.

I pull my long black coat tight with my right hand, while holding the cake carrier in my left. My heart pounds fiercely as I reach for the doorknob on his office door. Just as I turn the knob, I hear a woman's voice laughing. I freeze in my tracks.

I shake my head and tell myself that Reese would never cheat on me. He wouldn't hurt me like that. He couldn't be that awful, could he?

Then I hear the woman again, "Oh, baby. Please don't stop."

A thud sounds on the tile floor of the outer office as I drop the cake carrier. I stand like a statue. My feet feel like cement blocks. My mind yells at me to run. But I don't. My body moves toward where the woman's voice came from.

When I enter the main room of Reese's office, I see them in an embrace.

I turn and leave Defense Dynasty for the last time.

In my SUV, I slam my hands against the steering wheel. I'm shattered. My head falls back against the headrest as my breath catches in my lungs. How did I not know Reese was cheating on me? How did I miss the signs? Fuck! I'm such a fool. Never again.

Fuck it! I want to see Elio.

At home, I gather myself and take a calming shower. The hot water washes away the pain I witnessed at Reese's office. After showering, I slip into something comfortable, and fix myself a chamomile tea.

Opening my phone, I pan to Elio's name and type in a message. I don't click send though. My breathing quickens with the thought of taking this step. Of actually inviting another man to my house...

Laying my phone on the table, I press my hands against my cheeks and blow out a deep breath.

This isn't right, and I know it. Even though Reese cheated on me, at least it appeared as though he had, we're still married. I would be cheating on him if Elio comes over. But being unhappy, unloved, and lonely isn't right either. I don't know what to do as I stare at the message I wrote. My pulse pounds in my throat. My body tenses. I retype a new message for Elio.

> Me: Hi. I think the new AC unit isn't working right. Will you come by and check it?

A few minutes pass before the text bubbles percolate on my phone screen.

> Elio: I'll be right over.

Walking up to her house with my toolbox, my heart pounds like a fucking jack hammer. The excitement travels through me like lightning. My cock throbs, wanting to be inside her so badly.

She's older than me. A lot older. I'm not sure by exactly how much, but I think twenty years or more. I've never been with a woman older than me. It's a fantasy of mine, although I never thought I'd ever fulfill it… until I met her. She radiates joy and kindness. Her empathy towards me was evident when her husband was irritated with the air-conditioning unit being broken. Her beauty is truly both inside and out. She's perfect. Perfect for me.

The door opens, and there she is. My heart hammers. My breathing intensifies. She's a vision dressed in a thin, strapped, simple black jumper. The neckline dips deep, giving me a peek of her voluptuous breasts. She is the woman of my dreams.

"Hey," she says.

"Hi, gorgeous." I step closer to her, reaching for her hand.

She avoids my hand by crossing her arms, and asks, "Will you check the AC, please?"

"Of course." I grab my toolbox and head out to the outside compressor. When I remove the cover, I notice a loose wire and reattach it. The compressor begins to run, so I place the cover back on and secure it.

I return to the kitchen, and place my toolbox on the counter. Roxi leans against the small nook table, her head bowed.

"It was just a loose wire. It's all good now, Miss Roxi," I say as I step closer to her.

She sniffles, then tightens her arms across her chest. "Thank you," she whispers without looking at me.

With two fingers, I touch her chin and lift it so I can see her face. Her eyes are bloodshot. Her cheeks are splotchy. She bites her lip as she avoids looking at me.

Something inside me urges me to make her happy again. To take her sadness away, and fill it with joy. With love.

I wrap my arms around her waist, pulling her closer. Leaning down to kiss her soft lips, I kiss her cheek instead when she presses her face against my chest, avoiding me. I lift her head with two fingers on her chin, then lean down again, pressing my lips to hers. As I slide my tongue along her lips, she opens her mouth wide, and I get my first taste of sweet Roxi Remington.

She breaks our kiss quickly, pushing me away from her. She hides her face from me as her long blonde hair hangs down. I brush it away, placing my fingers on her chin again. Tilting her face up. Her blue eyes fill with desire and fear. I lean down, brushing my lips across hers tenderly. I whisper, "It's okay, beautiful."

"I'm married…"

"Shh, baby. Don't think. I want you to just feel. Let me

take care of you." I step closer. "C'mon, gorgeous. I'm dying to please you. Let me show you how a man's supposed to take care of his wife."

She turns her back to me.

I wrap my arms around her and lean down, nuzzling my mouth into her neck. Breathing deeply, I take all of her in. She smells like flowers. I kiss her neck and slide the straps of her jumper down her arms, then slide my hand up her camisole she has on underneath her jumper, cupping her soft breast.

She leans into me, moaning, "Oh, my god." A heavy breath escapes her as she allows me to turn her to face me.

Cupping her face, I kiss her deeply. Tasting all of my sweet Miss Roxi.

We kiss long and deep for several minutes as I walk her back into the living room. She leans back on the sofa as I kneel on the floor between her legs. Placing my hands on her bare calves, I slide them under her skirt, bunching it up around her hips. Moving her panties to the side, I kiss her pussy tenderly before licking her.

"Oh god, Elio," she pants.

My cock's a brick as I continue pleasing Roxi. Making her feel her bliss is my goal. I love hearing her moan out my name as she soaks my face.

"Elio! Jesus, don't stop. Oh my god," I pant as my AC-repair guy eats me for dinner. His soft lips kiss my clit. He kisses my pussy lips. His tongue caresses me. I've never been eaten like a precious delicacy. I need his mouth to make me purr, make me drench his soft beard and face.

My god, where has this beautiful young man been all my life? My legs tremble as I grab his strong arms, tugging hard as he continues licking me tenderly. My body erupts with cosmic celebrations as I come on his tongue. He doesn't stop though. A delicate kiss on my clit again, then his mouth sucks all of me up. My legs drape over his broad shoulders as he licks and kisses my cunt. I've died and gone to erotic heaven. I don't want him to stop, but my next orgasm explodes inside me, making me scream, "Fuck, Elio! Elio!"

He brings me to my second, third, fourth – I lose count orgasm with his beautiful, perfect mouth. No one has ever fucking done that to me. I was with several men before getting married, but never fucking ever has any man, including Reese, made me come with only his mouth and glorious tongue.

I catch my breath as my body quivers. I moan his name, not wanting him to stop devouring me. "Elio, Elio. Oh my god, baby."

He stretches up with his thick arm, grasping my breasts with his big, soft hand, tenderly kneading one after the other. I come completely undone again.

I glance around, wondering if I've died and gone to heaven, but no, we're in the house I share with my husband, who never thinks of me. Unlike the thirty-six-year-old lapping me up like he's starving and I'm his favorite meal.

"Mmm, beautiful, you're so delicious," Elio says as he leans over me, pressing his mouth to mine. I taste myself on his soft lips. His beard and mustache are wet from me. We kiss deeply for several minutes, then he stands and picks me up, carrying me into my bedroom.

He pushes me back onto the king-sized bed. I gaze at this large, grizzly bear-like man as he starts to strip. He's stout, with broad shoulders. Tanned skin, with a smattering of soft brown chest hair. No six-pack, more like a full barrel of all man, and I'm here for it. I love a big-all-over man. Abs are overrated. My eyes lock onto his thick erection. A smile tugs on my lips as I run my tongue around them. Fuck, I want him inside me. I want to suck his cock.

He lies on top of me gently. Then glides his hard cock inside me. I arch my back, pressing my breasts against his chest as he enters me slowly. His brown eyes meet my blue ones.

Elio leans down, covering my mouth with his, sliding his tongue inside while he plunges his dick into my needy cunt.

"Oh, fuck," I pant. "Jesus, Elio. Don't stop, baby." I kiss him deeply as he fucks me senseless. My pussy walls clench his hard cock. He pulls out, coming just above my clit.

I flip over, shoving my ass upward, wanting Elio to fuck

me again. He grabs my hips and sits up, pulling me back against him. He rubs his dick along my ass crack. I tense as I wonder if he'll fuck me there, but he doesn't. He just teases me.

My legs quiver as he pushes inside my pussy from behind. The sensations from this position bring another wonderful orgasm on full steam as he rocks my body against his, back and forth so fast. My head hangs; my heart races rapidly. I collapse onto the bed. "Oh my lord," I pant as I roll onto my back.

He stretches out beside me, caressing my hair from my face. "You're so beautiful, Roxi. So gorgeous, my love." He leans in, kissing my shoulder, then finding my lips.

I move closer to him as our kiss deepens, then lay my head on his chest when he lies back on the pillows, his one arm behind his head. He places his other hand on my head, guiding me toward his fat cock.

I've never sucked a man after he's been inside me, but I don't hesitate for a second. I take him in my mouth, making him hard again. I pull off before he comes.

He holds my chin and asks, "Wanna ride me, baby?"

My pussy clenches in wonderful anticipation of mounting his hard cock. I quickly crawl onto this hulk of a man, spread my legs, and sit myself down.

"Oh god," I cry as I slide onto him. Whipping my head wildly, I go for the ride of my life. I slap his thick chest, bouncing my ass as fast as I can.

He halts my rapid pace. "Slow down. I want to enjoy you." He cups my face, and brings me to him. We kiss deeply as I hold his cock inside me, wanting to feel him there for as long as possible.

Fuck, he feels so goddamn good. I don't want this to ever end.

It's time to put myself first.
Time to be completely happy in life.
Time to tell Reese I want a divorce.

Drenched

As I'm heading out to the pool in my bikini for a refreshing and cooling swim, my phone pings. I stop before going outside and glance at it, seeing a text from Lindsey. She's one of my best friends and part owner of SILK, the spa I go to for some quality 'me time.'

Lindsey: I hate to be that someone, but did you know about this?

A photo follows her text.

Grabbing my chest, I fall to the floor as I see my husband, Martin, in the arms of his paralegal.

I blink quickly, but when I look at my phone again, the photo is still there. My breath hitches and stops briefly as my mind runs in a million directions. This could be innocent. Just a congratulatory embrace for Lisa finally passing the bar. Maybe he's consoling her for something. *Or, fuck! Maybe he's cheating on you again,* my inner voice says.

I stare at the photo. Lisa's smiling and is much younger than me. Thinner, but I'm not out of shape by any means. I take care of myself. Eat right and exercise daily. I have lines on my face, whereas hers is like porcelain. Mine was like that at that age too. Life will get to her one day. I look closer at the photo and notice Martin is smiling wide with his arms around his newest whore.

A tear splashes on my cell phone screen just as Lindsey's next text appears.

Lindsey: Hey. Call me. Are you alright?

Me: I'm okay. I'll call later.

Lindsey: Okay. You better be or I'll come over. I've got you, Layne.

Me: I am. I promise. And thank you.

Lindsey: Always. Be strong.

I close the texts from Lindsey and open Martin's thread. I send him a text and include the photo.

Me: What the fuck?

My phone rings immediately.

"Layne, no. It's nothing. I swear. She's nothing. That photo is nothing," Martin promises without even saying hello. His rapid statements make me think it is everything I fear.

"Nice try, Martin. I know Lisa is your paralegal. What I don't know is why the fuck she's in your arms!" I scream into the speaker of my cell phone.

"Um, I don't even remember when that was taken. Anyway, who sent that to you? Was it Dottie? Scarlett? Fuck, Layne. It's nothing. I swear, baby."

"Shut up, just shut the fuck up. You want that. Young,

thin, pretty. Fuck you, Martin. I gave you everything. I worked to get you through law school. I gave up everything when I got pregnant, then stayed home with the twins. I…" I curl into a ball on the carpeted floor of our living room. My heart lies in pieces inside my chest. I'm breathing. I'm still alive, but my life is shattered.

"Layne, please. I'm coming home."

"No, don't."

"Layne, please. God, please don't say anything to the girls until I explain it all."

"Do you actually think I'll hurt our children like that?" I ask.

"No. Let me explain. You don't understand," he begs.

"No, I don't."

"I'll be there as soon as I can. I love you, Layne. I swear—"

"I won't be here," I lie. "So don't bother pretending to care anymore. I know it's fake." I hang up the phone, staring at the ceiling fan spinning round and round. My heart aches as it shatters inside my chest.

The intense pain coursing through me is more about my kids. My twin girls, Ruthie and Ruby. What will they say? How will they feel about their father when they find out what he's done to our family? To me?

I blink, and the tears trail down my cheeks. I won't hurt them. They love Martin. He's been a great dad to them. He loves them. But how can he be a good dad and a cheating husband? My mind spins, trying to make sense of this. My girls are my world. I can't hurt them. I can't break their hearts like their father broke mine. I won't.

I have new clients today. Martin and Layne Dawson. They live in the richest neighborhood here in South Beach. The Beau Monde Estates.

From reading the incoming report, the Dawsons are unhappy with how their pool and jacuzzi are being cleaned. At Pristine Pools Plus, we pride ourselves on being the best. Your pool is our pool, and we take care of it as such.

As I approach the guardhouse, I note the lush landscaping. Lots of palm trees and bushes. And several flowering plants like blazing stars, coral beans, milkweed, and passion-flower. The colors blend perfectly.

The guard stops me and asks, "Who are you here to see?"

"The Dawsons." I show him the email with the proposal for the pool service.

He squints at my phone, then scans the list of what I assume are the homeowners. He says, "You're good." He nods and presses a button.

The gates swing open, and I drive inside. My eyes widen at the sight of these enormous homes before me. Each one is a two-story building. Some have three and four car garages.

They all have immaculate lawns and matching mailboxes with lamps on top.

While I'm used to working on pools at these types of homes, these are even more prestigious than what I've taken care of so far.

I pull onto the brick paver driveway of the Dawson's home. Hopping out of my truck, I grab my backpack with all the paperwork in it for them to sign. I ring the doorbell and wait.

"Oh… Um, who are you?" a stunning brunette with blue eyes says. She's wearing a red bikini and a white sheer robe that hangs open. My eyes trail up and down her body, noticing her long, sleek, tan legs. Her nearly perfect midriff. Her full breasts. My dick throbs as I take in this beauty before me.

Bringing my eyes back to hers, I say, "I'm Beckett with Pristine Pools Plus. We're taking over the weekly upkeep of your pool and jacuzzi." I pull the contract from my backpack hanging off my shoulder. "I'm here to have the contract signed. I think Mr. Dawson set up this appointment last week." I smile, handing her the papers.

She takes them and looks the contract over. Handing them back, she says, "You'll need to speak with Martin. He's not here."

"Well, Mrs. Dawson—"

"It's Layne. Please call me Layne." A tiny smile tugs at her full and luscious lips.

"Okay. Layne." My body tingles after saying her name. "You may sign the contract. You're the owner too, right?" My brows lift as I hold out the contract for her, hoping she reconsiders and lets me in.

She reaches for the paper; her hand grazes mine. Our eyes meet for a second, causing my cock to twitch in my shorts again. She's breathtakingly gorgeous, and I can't take my eyes off her.

Suddenly, her eyes dart from mine, and she lets go of the papers. "Shit!" she hisses, then slams the door in my face.

"Layne! Layne, darling. Please…"

An older man –Mr. Dawson, I assume– rushes toward me. He ignores me as he tries to open the front door.

I step off the tiled porch and watch the drama unfolding in front of me.

He knocks on the wood and calls out, "Layne, please let me in. We need to talk. C'mon. Open the goddamn door!" He continues pounding.

Deciding this isn't my business, I get in my truck and leave the Dawson residence.

"Darling, please. Open the door. For Christ's sake. Let me explain." Knocking persists as I listen to Martin begging me to allow him in. I changed the lock code, which he realizes as soon as he jabs in our old number, only for it to beep in refusal. As he lets off a stream of curses, I stare at the glass door, realizing I don't want to hear anything he says. I don't want to fix this anymore.

This isn't Martin's first-time cheating. He cheated a year into our marriage. I'd just found out I was pregnant when he confessed to his infidelity. He begged me to forgive him. He promised to be the perfect husband and the best dad. I wasn't sure, but I didn't want to raise a baby on my own. It took a while, but I forgave Martin. I gave him a second chance. A couple of months later we found out I was having twins. I thought then I'd made the right decision forgiving Martin.

He was the perfect husband and father for the longest time, then he slipped up again, and I tried looking the other way when he messed with another one of his paralegals. She left the firm and never said a word. I'm sure Martin paid her handsomely to keep their secret.

Our girls were about ten that time. Maybe it was his ten-year itch. I don't know and at that time, I didn't care. I kicked him out. I wasn't going to be that type of wife who lets her husband cheat and keeps turning the other cheek. What's the saying; fool me once, shame on you, fool me twice, shame on me.

We were separated for a year.

Martin saw our girls on the weekends. But as the days, weeks, and months went on, I noticed my girls' sadness grew. Their grades dropped. Notes were sent home by their teachers about their behavior. I knew I had to do something, and that something was putting my family back together for my girls. So, I called Martin and invited him to move back into our home.

I stayed married to him to protect my babies. I know now what a mistake that was. Ruthie and Ruby will be devastated when they hear their father is a cheat.

I made him promise on our twins' lives that he'd never cheat again. He promised. Yet, here we are. What's the other old saying? Once a cheater, always a cheater? Fuck me. I should've listened.

Fuck. Fuck, Fuck.

I can't let him back into my life. Not without something from him. More than a stupid promise that I know he'll break. He's weak.

I can't live with a cheater. I can't live with a liar. I can't let him shatter my heart again. He's done it too many times already. I should've been stronger all those years ago. I should've left him and raised my girls on my own. I should've done everything differently. But it's too late for all of that. I'll make Martin pay for his betrayal. I'll make him pay for hurting me again. And he'll pay for breaking our family apart.

He tries to look through the glass, but it's glazed and he can't see me clearly. I turn away, ready to walk upstairs and throw his shit out the window.

"Layne. Jesus. Think of the girls. Please. Please."

I stomp toward the front door. Swinging it open, I bite at him, "Do not use the girls as a way to get to me." I shake my index finger at him. "You fucked up for the last time. Leave Ruthie and Ruby out of this mess." I spin and walk away from him.

"Layne, please." He follows me and grabs my arm, jerking me around to face him.

Yanking myself free, I hiss, "Never touch me again."

"It's not what you think," he says, hanging his head in shame.

"Really? What the hell is it then, Martin? Did you fuck her? Are you fucking her? Does she get on her knees like you want her to? Does she obey you?" I scream. "What. The. Fuck. Is. It?" I smack my hands together after each word to make him look at me.

Martin paces the entryway for several minutes as I glare at him with heat in my eyes. He rubs the back of his neck, then scratches his face with both hands.

"Martin!" I yell.

His head falls to his chest. He puffs out a breath, then says, "I'm sorry, Layne. I'm so sorry."

"Sorry for what, Martin? Getting caught? Fucking her? Lying to me? To our girls? What?" I demand, my hands on my hips.

He shakes his head, then raises his eyes to mine. A long, uncomfortable silence sits between us. He plops onto one of the foyer chairs. "All of it, Layne. All of it." He looks away and drags his hands through his short brown hair.

"So what now, Martin? What do we do now?" I ask, tears

pricking my eyes. I don't want to cry over a cheating husband. I don't need him to survive. We didn't sign a prenup. I get half of every goddamn thing we own. I'm not worried about myself. I'm worried about my girls. The fallout from Martin's infidelity will crush them. He's their hero. They've always been Daddy's girls. My heart slows as the pain of my husband's latest affair drains me. Striding into the kitchen, I go to the liquor cabinet. I grab a tumbler and a bottle of Macallan to make myself a whiskey neat. He follows me, and as I turn around, I ask, "What now?"

"I don't know. Do you want a divorce? I failed you. Is there anything I can do to make this right?" he asks.

"You need to make it right with our daughters. We're done. But *you* must tell Ruthie and Ruby everything. This clusterfuck is all on you, Martin. I'll be here for them. But I'm done with you." I toss back my drink. "Figure it out and fast." I spin on my heels, then remember why I was at the door in the first place and turn back around. "The new pool company sent its guy here to have the contract signed. That's coming out of your half of the fucking finances."

"Layne." Martin grabs my arm.

"What?" I lift one eyebrow and look at his hand on my arm.

He lets go of me. "Let me speak with Ruthie and Ruby before kicking me out. I promise to talk to them this weekend. Please, Layne," he begs.

Thinking of my daughters' feelings only, I agree to let Martin stay until the weekend. "Tell them everything. And I mean every fucking thing. I'll take care of them after you hurt them with your ugly truth." I turn away, leaving my shitbag, cheating husband to wallow in his regret.

That was the most uncomfortable first meeting with a new client I've ever experienced. On the way to my next client's house, my phone pings with a text from Mrs. Dawson.

> Layne: Mr. Beckett. We've decided to hire Pristine Pools Plus. Do you have time to come back by our house today?

> Me: Great news. I can come back in a few hours.

> Layne: Perfect.

I call my boss and give him the good news. I finish up with my other clients before heading back to the Dawson's.

Layne answers the door, still in her red bikini. Fuck she looks amazing. I do all I can to not drool or stumble over my words.

My heart hammers as I breathe deep to control my damn cock from becoming a brick. My tank-top doesn't quite hang long enough to cover the visible bulge growing in my shorts.

"Ah, Mr. Beckett. Thank you so much for coming back. Come in." She reaches for my arm, and leads me into the entryway.

"It's just Beckett. And you're welcome. I aim to please," I say, and glance around looking for Mr. Dawson.

"Come with me, please." Layne tugs on my arm, and I follow her through the massive house to the living room. There're huge sliding glass doors that lead out to the lanai where the pool and jacuzzi are. She stops and turns to face me. "When you're finished with the pool, I have a proposition for you."

I cock an eyebrow, and my dick hardens. "May I ask what kind of proposition you have in mind, Layne?"

She trails her index finger along my bare bicep, circling the infinity tattoo I have there. She walks around me, dragging her finger across my back, stopping on my other bicep. She leans in and whispers against my ear, "I promise you'll like it, Beckett."

Her warm breath sends heated pulses through my body, causing my cock to harden. I need to adjust myself, but then I catch her gaze.

Her blue eyes sparkle. She licks her lips. "Mmm, mmm, mmm." She smiles, dropping her eyes to my obvious attraction to her.

"Ah, hold that thought, Layne. I need to clean your pool and jacuzzi."

"I'll be waiting for you upstairs on the deck," she says.

"What the hell is this for? Layne?" Martin whines.

I point to the chair and say, "Sit down and shut up."

"You're not serious." He shakes his head. "I'm not doing this." He folds his arms across his chest.

"Martin, darling. You don't have a choice. If you want any chance to stay in this marriage… Sit your ass down… Now!" I hiss.

"Hmph." He puffs out a breath, then reluctantly sits in the chair.

That wasn't too much of a fight from him, maybe he wants me to be more forceful with him. But that's not my personality. I prefer my man to dominate me. I'll switch it up today and see how much I like ordering him around.

"This is how our arrangement is going to work," I begin. "Since you've cheated on me three times. You owe me."

"What does that mean, Layne?"

"If you want to maybe stay married, I get to have a lover—"

"Layne, what the fuck are you saying? You're going to

cheat on me? For revenge? Seriously?" Martin stares up at me in disbelief. "And what do you mean 'maybe'?"

"I'll decide afterwards." I nod. "Yes. That's exactly what my offer is to you. If you want a chance to stay married to me, I get to be with whomever I choose. And you're going to know when it takes place." I bring the duct tape out from behind my back that I was hiding from him. "Sit still—"

"What the fuck? No, Layne. You're not taping me to this chair." He bolts to his feet, nearly knocking me over.

I grasp the doorframe and regain my balance. Heat rises up my neck. I knew he'd be a pain in my ass. Thinking back, he's been that most of our marriage.

I shove him hard with both hands on his chest, pushing him back down onto the chair.

"Sit the fuck down and shut the fuck up. I told you that you don't have a choice. If you want any chance of staying married to me; if you want to live in this house with me and our girls... Sit. Your. Ass. Down. Shut. Your. Mouth. And enjoy the show that you're about to hear." I step closer to him as he shifts in the chair. My hands are on my hips, my eyes glare fire through Martin. I've had enough from him and I need to get ready for Beckett.

Martin sits slumped in the chair. His mouth turned down. His eyes are glassy. I may have seen a tear sliding down his cheek. I shrug it all off and secure him to the chair with duct tape around his wrists and his ankles. I make sure the tape isn't too tight on him that would stop any blood flow, or leave marks. I'm not a monster. I just want some sweet revenge on my asshole of a husband.

Once finished, I stand and run my hand along his cheek. I smile wide and say, "Relax, Martin, while our new pool guy fucks me like crazy when he's done cleaning the pool today."

His eyes are wide as he shakes his head, but that slight tug on his lips is back. He likes this, he's just playing a role. "Layne—" There's a hint of a grin tugging on the corners of his lips.

Fuck, I think he does like this. I raise my hand to shush him. "It's not negotiable, Martin. You're going to listen to Beckett and me have sex. You don't have a choice." I tap his forehead. "Well, you do have a choice. It's this or move out."

"Layne, please," he whines through a small grin.

"Enjoy the show. I know I will."

"I can't believe you're making me do this," he fake pouts as his smile grows.

I play along, being the scorned wife that I am. "Seriously? You can't believe me? You did this. This is all your doing." I blow him a kiss, then just to rub it in further, I say, "Enjoy this younger man fucking your wife." I turn and walk into our bedroom, leaving the door ajar. I go out onto the deck and wait for Beckett to join me.

"Well, aren't you a gorgeous sight?" I say, walking toward Layne stretched out on a lounge chair on the deck outside her bedroom. The French doors are wide open. The king-sized bed is neatly made with three layers of fancy pillows. I plan on making a mess of them when I have my way with her.

"Hey, handsome. Come here. I want to explain the arrangement to you." She pats the end of the lounge chair as she curls her long, toned legs under her. She's fucking stunning.

I sit, adjusting my stiff cock as I do. It's ready to fuck her senseless, but I want to hear this thing she has planned for us.

"I'm all ears." I smile and lean closer to her.

"In all seriousness. If you don't want to do this, you may refuse me. But I hope you'll play along." She sits forward and places a hand on my arm.

"If it means having you, I'm all in, babe." I place my hand over hers and give it a soft squeeze.

She bites her lip, then says, "Okay, Beckett. You see, my husband has cheated on me a few times. This last time I found out about it, I decided he had to pay a price other than groveling for my forgiveness." She pauses and glances into her bedroom.

"And…" I push for more information.

"He has to listen to us fucking," she states as she sits tall in the lounge chair. A mischievous grin fills her face.

"Okay. How does that work? Is he in the room with us, blindfolded? Is he in another room listening through the wall?" I ask.

"Actually, he's taped to a chair just outside my bedroom door." She leans closer to me and whispers, "I think he might just like hearing me get fucked by another man."

"No way. Really?" My mouth half drops to the floor as I think there's no way I'd want to hear another man fucking my woman. Never, ever, ever.

She nods and smiles wide. "Yes. My bedroom door is slightly open. Martin is securely and safely taped to the chair. He's fine. So, Beckett. Are you okay with this?" she asks.

"Yes. Anything to be with you, Layne." I lean into her and kiss her full lips softly. I move back and say, "If you were mine, this would never happen. I'd never cheat on you."

She slides her hands around my neck. Locking her fingers, she tugs me closer and smashes her lips to mine. Her tongue pushes between my lips and finds my tongue. Our bodies tangle for a few minutes on the lounge chair.

Standing, I hold a hand for her and she takes it. I sweep her off her feet and carry her into her bedroom. Seeing the bedroom door open a bit, I beam with excitement for what's about to happen.

I place my hand in his and think, *mmm, Beckett*. He's not your typical pool guy. He's stout and grizzly, more of a mountain man type than a Florida boy. But there's something about this not-so-perfect younger man that has me wanting him. Maybe because he's the complete opposite of my cheating husband.

Gently lying me on the bed, he slides his hands up my bare thighs. Finding my bikini bottom, he hooks his index fingers on each side, and pulls it down my legs, then tosses it aside.

He falls to a knee and plants a kiss on my calf, then my inner thigh.

"Oh, dear god," I pant as his lips trail closer to my pussy. It craves his soft lips, the tickle of his mustache and beard. Who knew facial hair felt so fucking good?

"Mmm, Layne. You're delicious, and so damn wet," Beckett breathes against my pussy lips, making me quiver with pleasure. He continues his feast on me as I moan and come on his face more than once. He holds my thighs firmly with his big powerful hands so I can't escape him.

I don't want to escape him at all, but he's pushed me over the edge so many times. I've never been someone's favorite meal like I am his. He doesn't stop licking, sucking, kissing my pussy for what feels like forever.

My back arches deeper with each glorious orgasm he pulls from me. My head rolls from side to side. My breathing intensifies. I grip his arms tightly, digging my fingers in as he eats me into oblivion.

"Jesus, Beckett!" I squeal when I've come undone again. "You're so goddamn amazing," I squeeze my legs around his head.

He kisses my pussy tenderly before standing. It's like he's telling it, he'll be back soon. Raising my legs, he crosses my ankles, then drags me to the edge of the bed. Spreading me wide, he shoves his hard, thick cock into me.

"Baby, you feel so good," he moans as he thrusts in and out of me rapidly.

Our eyes meet in the throes of passion. His deep browns dance with heat. Mine close on a scream. Grabbing my tits, I squeeze them as Beckett fucks me crazy.

He lays my legs down on the bed as he leans closer to me as his cock plunges deeper inside me.

I reach up and rub the drops of my cum into his mustache and beard.

He looks into my eyes and says too low for Martin to hear, "I'll save that for later." His mouth covers mine, kissing me passionately. Our tongues devouring the other.

I wrap my legs around his waist and lock my ankles, pulling him even deeper inside my pussy. Fuck, he feels glorious as he fills me up with his thick cock.

"My god, Beckett!" I scream as he pulls another orgasm from me. My hips buck upward to meet his.

After several minutes of incredible fucking, Beckett calls

out, "Fuck, Layne. I'm coming. Oh, baby. Fuck!" His body stiffens and he pushes in as deep as my body allows. He grips my shoulders tightly and buries his head against my shoulder.

I turn my head and kiss his cheek. "You're amazing," I whisper and kiss him again.

He turns his head to face me. Smiling wide, he whispers back, "And you're the woman I've been searching for all my life." He kisses my mouth hard, then falls to my side.

A bit stunned by Beckett's statement, I lie on my back, staring at the ceiling. Do I take a chance with this younger man, who I don't know much about other than he's fucking magnificent in bed. He seems dependable. He's sexy as fuck.

Do I want to stay married to my cheating husband or take a chance on something with Beckett?

Layne

Beckett leaves after taking a quick shower.

I stand before Martin and take the scissors to cut him free.

"It's about damn time. Jesus, Layne." He rubs his wrists for affect, but I know he wasn't taped tight enough to hurt him or leave any marks. He's such a drama bitch.

I puff out a breath and say, "I don't want to do this anymore."

"Wait, what do you mean? You don't want to have sex with another man and make me listen?" he asks.

I go back into our bedroom and make the bed.

"Hey," Martin says. "Aren't you going to wash the sheets?"

I shake my head and finish tucking the comforter under the pillows. "Nope."

"Why? I don't want to lay where *he* was."

"Oh, do not worry about that, Martin. You're never laying in this bed again. When I said I didn't want to do this anymore; I meant us." I wag my finger between him and me.

"But, wait. That wasn't the deal. You said—"

"Fuck what I said. I changed my mind." I fold my arms under my breasts.

"That's not fair, Layne. I only agreed to hear him fuck you to save our marriage," Martin bites out at me.

"I don't want an audience. You did what you did, now it's time to pay the ultimate price for your betrayal. How do I know you only cheated the three times I caught you? Is there more, Martin?" I ask.

He turns away from me. His shoulders slump and he plops onto the chaise at the end of our bed. He swallows hard.

"Martin. I'm right, aren't I? You've cheated more than just the three times I caught you." I stand in front of him as he fidgets with his hands.

Silence floats heavy between us as I wait for him to answer me. His silence tells me everything I need to know. I deserve better.

My husband doesn't speak his confession. He nods his head and sighs heavily.

Fed up and tired of living this life, I say, "You have a week to get out. During that week, you'll sleep in one of the guest rooms. I don't give a fuck which one, but stay out of this room. This room is mine. This house is mine. I'll file for divorce," I say calmly. Inside though, my blood boils finding out he cheated more than I knew. I don't want to know the exact amount of times he cheated or with whom, but I'm done. I want out. "Please leave now." I don't look at him as I point toward the bedroom door.

Martin stands. He opens his mouth to speak, then turns from me and walks out of our bedroom.

I walk out onto the deck and breathe in the warm, fresh air. I pick up my phone from the table it lays on and thumb to Beckett's number.

Me: Can't wait to see you again.

Beckett: I'm all yours. Whenever you want me. ❤️ 😘

Me: ❤️ 😘

Plugged

"**G**ood morning, babe." I slide my hand under the sheet and down Damien's chest. It's been too long since my husband has had a nice morning wood for me to ride. I grasp his stiff cock and scoot closer to him, kissing his scruffy cheek.

"Jesus, Khloe. What the hell?" He grabs my hand, stopping me from stroking him.

"Aw, baby. I want some of this, please," I beg as I try to grasp his dick again.

He quickly sits up, turning away from me. "Fuck, Khloe. Your breath stinks in the morning. You know that."

"I can go freshen up –"

"I can't. I have an early meeting with a new client." He scratches his beard, then turns away from me. Standing, he walks into our bathroom, closing the door behind him.

"Fuck," I blurt out. If he won't satisfy me, I'll take care of myself. Reaching to my left, I yank open the nightstand drawer and pull out the bottle of lube, my pink vibrator, and the nice thick dark-pink dildo. Sliding my panties off, I lie back on the pile of pillows behind me and begin my morning masturbation session that's become a regular routine for the past six months or so, since Damien is *too busy* for me.

Lifting my ass a bit, I slide the dildo into my pussy. "Fuck me. God, this feels so good. But not as good as the real thing. Hmph," I whine aloud.

Pressing the button on the vibrator, I hold it steady on my clit as I plunge the dildo in and out of me. My hips buck in rhythm as my arousal rises. It doesn't take long before I'm about to come on the fake dick inside me, wishing it were Damien's. Or at this point, any man.

"Oh my god!" I scream.

"Christ, Khloe!" Damien scoffs as he steps out of the bathroom, a towel wrapped around his waist. He looks disgustingly at the vibrator lying on the bed. "You couldn't wait until after I went to work to fuck yourself?"

My neck heats. Blood rushes behind my ears. I stand in all my naked glory and yell, "No! Damien. I couldn't fucking wait. I have needs. Wants. Desires. I want you!" I stomp around the end of our bed and toward him. Poking his firm chest with my index finger, I say, "But you're always too goddamn busy. Your work takes precedence over me all the fucking, goddamn time. Your obligations to me as your wife obviously don't matter anymore. Don't you want me?" I huff out a breath, then drag my hand through my hair.

"Don't be so emotional, Khloe."

"Hmph." I puff out a frustrated breath. "I'm tired of fucking myself for the last several months. I'm tired of eating dinner alone most nights. I'm tired of making excuses to our friends when they invite us out. I'm fucking tired of it all, Damien!" I push past him and retrieve my robe on the hook in the bathroom. "If you don't want me anymore, maybe I should find myself a boyfriend," I state, glaring at him with fury and a confidence I've not had before.

Damien steps away from me, shaking his head. "I can't believe you'd say that. I'm sorry for trying to provide a great life for you by working. No, wait. By being a highly successful partner in Defense Dynasty. Making sure you have everything you need. Not wanting for anything."

"Except a bit of intimacy," I say without hesitation, standing in the doorway of the closet, my hands on my hips.

"Seriously, Khloe? What the fuck? That's the reason you're behaving like this? Because I've not fucked you in…" He looks up at the ceiling as if counting.

"In over six months, Damien. Six long months. You barely even kiss me. Or hold me. Why are we still married if you don't want to be intimate with me like husbands and wives are?"

"I didn't know I had to perform in a certain timeframe," he yells, his face red with anger. "I didn't know I had to fill a sex quota for you!" He pushes me aside to get into the closet.

"It's not a quota, asshole. It's our marriage I'm trying to save. But since you can't seem to find any time for me, maybe I will find a boyfriend. Hmph." I blow out a breath, and he turns on me with a snide smile.

"Go ahead. Throw yourself at as many men as you want. Because all you're going to find is no one is going to want to fuck a washed-up, old, ugly bitch like you."

I stumble back in pain, wondering how the hell we got here. How long has he hated me? Maybe since the beginning?

Fuck. Now I know being forced to marry me all those years ago after his grandfather stated in his will that Damien's inheritance was contingent on him being married, was a bad idea. Although I'd had a crush on Damien all through high school, I was thrilled when he proposed. He told me about his grandfather's stipulation after we wed. He swore it wasn't the real reason he asked me to marry him. He swore he loved me and wanted to spend all of his life with me. Young and naïve Khloe believed every word he fed me.

After this morning's spew of hateful words, I know now, I was used as a pawn to get his hands on that money. Yeah, fuck him. I don't need him.

After my husband leaves, I take a shower and wash the dildo at the same time. Afterwards as I'm sitting at the makeup table, the light flickers several times, then goes out.

"What the fuck now? This day cannot get any worse," I huff out. I stand to reach for the switch on the wall. Flick it several times. Nothing turns on. I check all the switches in the upstairs rooms. None of them work. I head downstairs, and all the switches turn on. *What the fuck?*

In the garage, I open the electrical panel. It's like looking at a million-piece puzzle, so I close it and return to the kitchen, where I find my phone and search for an electrician who can come here today.

"Good morning, Diego's Best Electricians," says the receptionist who answers my call. "This is Mary. How may I help you?"

"I need someone immediately, please. I've got no electricity upstairs. Please, can you send someone?"

"Um, let me check the schedule." Silence on the line for a few seconds, then she says, "Oh, yes, ma'am. I'll need your address. I'm sure I can get Diego out to your place in about an hour. Is that okay?"

"That's great. Thank you so very much." I give Mary my address, then wait for Diego to come to my home.

I t's been a slow week. Then an emergency call comes in. Mary texts me the address of a Khloe Stanton. She lives in the Beau Monde Estates, one of the richest neighborhoods here in South Beach.

I drive up to the security pavilion and tell the guard the address and name of my customer. He checks a monitor to his right, then nods, and raises the security gates.

Driving slowly, taking in all the enormous homes, I arrive at the Stanton's. The garage door slowly opens, and I wonder if the electricity came back. Grabbing my tool belt and back-pack, I step out of my truck when I notice her. My breath catches. My heartbeat quickens. My cock twitches. Fuck, she's drop-dead gorgeous, with her long red hair whipping in the summer breeze. She's wearing a white sundress and sandals.

"Oh, my god. Thank you for coming," she says as she extends her hand to me. "I'm Khloe."

I shake her hand and ask, "Did your electricity return?" I nod toward the open garage.

"Um, no. It's only the upstairs that doesn't have electricity. I've been after Damien to buy a whole-home generator for years, but he's a procrastinator. So now I need you to fix it." She smiles sweetly as she waves her arm toward the house.

Damien Stanton – why does that name sound familiar? I glance around the house, then it hits me. He's the big-shot defense attorney with Defense Dynasty. He defends the sleazy fuckers who pretend to make investments for people. The ones who make Ponzi schemes. I can't remember how many creeps he's gotten off with a slap on the wrist or no punishment at all. While the victims are financially destroyed.

Khloe seems too kind to have any idea that her husband is a sleazy white-collar criminal lawyer.

Turning my attention back to Khloe, I ask, "Will you show me the electrical panel first?"

"Sure. Follow me," she says, turning and heading back inside the garage.

I stare at her round ass as she walks ahead of me since the white dress she's wearing flies up with the breeze. Goddamn, I've never seen a more perfect ass. My cock agrees as it throbs in my work pants. I adjust myself before she sees my obvious attraction to her. But my eyes don't leave her ass until she says, "Here's the box."

"Oh, ah, thank you, Mrs. Stanton—"

She interrupts me, saying, "Oh, no, sir. It's Khloe. Please. Mrs. Stanton lives in Key West."

"Okay, Khloe." I open the panel door and look at the row of breakers. It's clear which one is faulty given its switch is in the off position. Pity, this might not be that long of a job at all…

"I'll be out by the pool if you need anything," she says.

"Got it. I'll let you know what I find here and what's wrong." I turn back to the panel to try to focus on the job at hand and not about how much I want that ass of hers.

Holy *shit!* When did electricians get so damn young and hot? It's been a long time since my husband's paid me any attention, and this gorgeous Latino was eating me with his big brown hunger-filled eyes.

I grab my phone, an e-reader from the counter, then water from the refrigerator on the lanai, and turn on my battery powered hand-held fan to try to cool off. Sitting in one of the lounge chairs, I open my e-reader to the latest romance book I'm in the middle of.

After a few chapters, I'm melting, so I pull off my sundress. Grabbing one of the long floating tubes, I slide it between my legs and walk into the cool pool water. I float up and down the thirty-foot-long pool. After a few minutes as I float in the refreshing pool, I hear Diego's voice call for me, "Khloe."

He steps out onto the lanai from the family room just as I'm toweling off. I smile when he says, "Wow."

Instead of wrapping the beach towel around me, I sling it over my shoulder. After months of being ignored by my husband and then being told this morning that he isn't even attracted to me anymore, I may as well give this hot Latino a full view.

A mischievous grin tugs at his mouth. He tries to cover his lips when he wipes his clean-shaven face. He's about six-foot and one-hundred-eighty-pounds. He's built similarly to Damien, but unlike my husband, Diego likes what he sees.

Placing my foot on the rim of the lifted jacuzzi, I bend over to slip on my sandal. I bend low, and my breasts practically spill out of my bikini top. I noticed him glancing at my ass earlier, but maybe he'll like my breasts too.

"Um… ah… Jesus," Diego stutters as he slides his hand through his short dark-brown hair.

Our eyes meet as I stand again. I run my tongue along the bottom on my teeth, then wet my lips before sliding my sunglasses on.

"Yes, Diego. What's wrong with my electricity? Can it be fixed quickly?" I walk toward him.

"Yes and –" He shrugs.

"Okay. I'm going to need more. Yes, you know what's wrong? And no, you can't fix it quickly?" I ask.

"Not quite. Let me show you." He holds his hand out, then drops it and says, "I'm sorry."

Grab that hand. You know you want to. You want more than just his hand, K.

A heated quiver rushing through me, I reach for his hand. Smiling, I say, "Lead the way."

He squeezes my hand and smiles wide. His brown eyes meet mine, filled with heat and carnal desire. He tugs on my arm, and I follow him through my house to the garage.

Diego

"**H**ere's the issue," I say and lift our hands to the breaker that was tripped.

The softness of her hand in mine has me thinking of how soft her body would feel under me. How much I want to eat her perfect ass.

"So what can you do about it?" she says, bringing my attention back to the electrical panel.

"I can just flip it back on. But… when I'm called out to a job, we charge a minimum of an hour's service. This will take only a few seconds to fix, so…" I step behind her and pull her away from the panel. Her ass presses against me, cushioning my already-hard cock. I quickly but gently push her from me.

"Mmm, so I have a full hour with you then?" she purrs, pushing her ass back against me.

Fuck, how I want her ass. This isn't what I normally do, but when opportunity knocks, I'm going to fucking answer it.

Leaning down, I kiss her shoulder.

Her head falls back against me, giving me access to her neck. I trail my lips along her soft skin, licking the pool water from her.

I'd noticed her swimming for a minute and thought about joining her in the pool, but then I remembered I was there to fix her electrical problems. My cock didn't care at all about why I was there. It wanted inside her ass.

I called her name and she swam to the shallow end. My cock throbbed hard in my shorts as she came out of the pool and dried herself off. Her tight body sent lightning bolts of heat through me. It's not just her round ass that has me wanting her. Her tits are perfect. I want all of her.

"Oh, dear god," she pants as I grab her large tits and squeeze. "Diego," she whispers.

"Khloe, should I stop?" I ask, hoping she says no.

She pushes her ass back more and says, "No, please don't stop."

I guide her to the door in the garage that leads inside to the kitchen.

She pulls me up the stairs and into her bedroom. I glance up as I follow her. Holy fuck, I want that ass.

Facing me, she slides her hand along my chest, then tugs on the hem of my polo. In seconds, we're naked and lying on the bed. Our lips smash together. She tastes like a cherry lollipop, my favorite flavor of candy.

After several minutes of kissing and groping, I say, "I want your ass, Khloe."

"Mmm, Diego. What will you do to my ass?" she asks as she glides her finger down my chest, over my abs, then circles the wet tip of my stiff cock.

Licking my lips, I say, "I want to eat your gorgeous ass, then I want to fuck your ass until you scream out my name in pleasure." My eyebrows bounce, and I caress her hip, sliding my hand onto her ass cheek.

She lies on her stomach and sticks her ass in the air. "All yours, big guy." She reaches around and spanks herself. She reaches for the nightstand, then opens the drawer. "Don't forget this." She hands me a bottle of lube and I take it.

My heart races like a freaking gazelle running from a lioness. Jesus, where has this fabulous woman been all my life? Most of the women I meet won't let me near their ass.

But I've always been an ass man. I love everything about it. Licking, poking, kissing, tonguing, and fucking it. Ass is my perfect fuck. Asses are so goddamn tight, and I love them.

Before I lube her up, I kiss each cheek, then slide my tongue up and down each one. I gently spread her ass cheeks apart, and my cock hardens even more at the sight of her hole. Leaning down, I slide my tongue along her ass crack. I stop and swirl it over her tight hole.

"Oh, fuck. Oh, Jesus," she cries out. "Wait. I need my vibrator."

She reaches over and opens the drawer on the nightstand. Then she pulls out a pink vibrator.

"If you're paying all your attention to my ass, I'm going to take care of my pussy." She lies back down on the bed, her ass in the air for me to resume my lunch.

"Mmm," I say after tasting her again. "Fuck, you're delicious." I smack her cheek just as she turns on the vibrator.

"God, yes," she pants as the hum of the vibrator sounds. She moves it over her pussy, then holds it on her clit.

I lick her ass, pressing my face deep between her soft cheeks. I dip my tongue into her as her vibrator hums beneath my chin. As my tongue feels how tight she is, my cock throbs hard, wanting in on the action. After a few minutes of munching on her ass, I sit up and open the lube.

"Fuck my ass, Diego." Khloe turns the vibrator on high.

Using a lot of lube, I press my dick against her, then pull

back. I know to take my time with her. I want her to enjoy this as much as I know I will, once I push all the way in.

"Again. Further. Now," she demands as her breathing quickens.

I grip her hips and push the tip of my cock inside her tight hole. As I rock my hips slowly, she pushes back slightly. My cock pulsates as I push in again. "Mmm, fuck. You're so goddamn tight, Khloe. Your ass is amazing."

We begin a slow, steady back-and-forth motion. Her asshole grabs my cock as I push and pull inside her. I can feel the vibrator as she runs it along her pussy, and it's bringing my orgasm on too fast.

"Fuck me harder, Diego. Fuck! Fuck! Fuck! Oh my god. Ah!" she squeals.

"You feel so fucking amazing," I groan as I speed up my rhythm. "You're driving me crazy, and I'm about to blow my load. Christ!" I yell as my body stiffens, and I come inside her before pulling out.

"Yes, baby, yes!" she screams and collapses onto the bed, then rolls onto her side.

I run my hand along my hip. Surprisingly, my ass feels great. I wasn't sure how it would feel since I've never had it fucked before. Damien would never even think of fucking me there. What am I saying? He doesn't even think of fucking my pussy anymore.

"You okay?" Diego asks as he lies beside me. His dark eyes are soft with lust.

"I'm great, baby. That was amazing." I lean close and brush his lips with mine.

He glides his big hand over my ass, spanking me softly. He grabs a fistful before leaning down to kiss my ass. "So, perfect." He sits on the end of the bed, then stands. "Mind if I take a shower so I can fuck you again?" He winks as he grabs his cock.

"I don't mind at all. It's through that door," I say, waving my arm toward the bathroom door.

"Don't move, sexy." Diego turns and walks into the bathroom.

I stare after him, enjoying the exquisite view of his tanned, muscular body.

He reaches into the shower stall and turns on the water. His plump ass faces me as I lay on my side. Licking my lips, I wait until he's inside the shower, then slither in behind him.

"Mmm," he moans as my hand finds his semi-hard cock.

"Let me help you shower and get your cock hard to fuck me again." I stroke his dick slowly from behind, then he takes my hand in his.

He spins to face me and places my hand back on his hard cock. He leans down, smashing his mouth to mine. His tongue pushes between my lips, finding mine.

We kiss long and hard as the water cascades over our bodies. He's hard as a brick as I continue stroking and cleaning him.

"Oh my god, Khloe. Fuck, babe," Diego groans.

Once he's clean, I drop to my knees and kiss the tip of his cock. I lick his shaft and roll his balls in my hand. Peering up at him just as I take his dick in my mouth, I move my hands to his ass, squeezing both cheeks.

"Holy fuck!" he yells. His hips begin to thrust against my face. Faster and faster for a few minutes, then he holds my head still. "I'm coming," he pants. "Fuck, I'm coming."

I open my throat and take Diego as deep as I can. He sprays jet after jet of warm cum down my throat. Once he's done, he releases my head. His dick falls from my mouth. He slides his hands under my arms and lifts me to standing as I lick my lips clean.

"Mmm. You are delicious, Diego," I say, and stand on my tiptoes to kiss him.

"You naughty minx. How am I supposed to fuck you again with this?" He holds his limp dick in his hands.

"I'll help you again, lover," I say with a sinful grin tugging my mouth upward.

"Oh, I have no doubt." He slides his hands around my

body, landing them on my ass. He squeezes both cheeks, then lifts me onto his firm body.

I wrap my legs around him, locking my ankles together and lacing my fingers around the nape of his neck.

Diego's passionate gaze fills me with desire. I've not been looked at like he looks at me in a long time.

I tug on his neck and smash my lips to his. Our tongues sliding in and out of each other's mouths. He tastes delicious.

Pulling back from our kiss when his cock pokes my ass cheek, I smile and bite my lip. "That didn't take long," I say, bouncing my body on his.

"You're so goddamn sexy, Khloe. I'll spend all day and night fucking you crazy."

"Promise?" I tease as I slide down onto his hard cock. "You feel just as good inside my pussy as you did in my ass." I kiss him deeply before he can reply. I don't want him talking. I want him fucking me until I can't walk.

Diego presses me against the cool shower tiles. He thrusts into me over and over as we kiss. I hold on for the ride of my life.

After several minutes of incredible sex, I say, "Finish me on my bed, baby."

"Your wish is my command," Diego says. He takes a step toward the shower door, still holding me on his body.

I push the glass door open, allowing him to walk toward my bed. Dropping me onto the king-sized bed, I scoot to the middle and pat the bed.

Diego crawls onto the bed. Before I know it, he's between my legs. He kisses my knees, then my inner thighs.

"You're driving me crazy," I pant. "Eat me and fuck me. Just don't make me wait."

"Mmm, yes ma'am." Diego licks his lips, then dives into my pussy. His tongue licks me from my tight hole to my clit. He tenderly kisses my pussy lips, and gently licks them.

"Oh god, Diego. Don't stop," I purr, holding his head in place. My hips push toward him, wanting him to go deeper with his magical tongue. "Yes, baby. Right there. Fuck!" I cry out when my orgasm comes on his tongue.

He lifts his head, smiling sinfully. He licks my cum from his lips as he crawls up my quivering body.

"You taste good, baby," he whispers against my cheek.

"You're amazing, Diego. So fucking amazing. I want—"

"What the fuck do you want, Khloe!" Damien yells, standing in the doorway of our bedroom.

Diego falls to my side and places his hand on my hip when I sit up on the side of the bed.

Glaring at my husband, my heart hammering, I tell him, "You don't want me anymore, so I found someone who does." I cross my arms.

"Khloe. Are you cheating on me with the help?" he whines, nodding toward Diego lying on the bed. "I didn't mean what I said this morning." He takes a step closer to me, reaching for me.

I slap his hand and say, "Fuck you, Damien. You said what you said. You can't take it back. Now get your shit and get out of here. We're done. Besides, Diego fucks me much better than you ever did."

Screwed

Dottie

W e met a few months ago when he came to fix the broken lock on my front door. Then it was the garage door opener, a leaking toilet, the gate to our fence outback, and once, he even repaired my car.

Ace repairs everything in my house. Anything I need done. One call, and he's there. He's never said no to me. One day, I asked him, "Don't you have a company to run? Or other customers to tend to?"

"I do, but you're always first on my list, honey." His smile was magnetic, his hazel eyes dancing when he looked at me.

Today, he's repairing the sink in my daughter's bathroom. If only he could fix me…

"Could you hand me the wrench in my bag?" Ace asks from under the vanity.

I look around and grab what I think is a wrench from his bag and offer it to him. "Here," I say.

A snort comes from him as he ducks his head and comes out from underneath the sink. He holds up the tool I thought was a wrench and says with a wide grin, "Honey, these are pliers. Close to a wrench but not quite." He stretches and grabs his tool bag, dragging it closer to him. His muscular, tanned arm flexes as he holds up another tool. "This is a wrench, Dottie."

I laugh, "Sorry for the mistake. I know nothing about tools. Thank you for showing me." My cheeks flush as he winks, then returns to his task.

I lean against the door frame, mesmerized by Ace's perfect physique. My mind wanders to how he'd feel on top of me. Embracing me. Kissing me. Fucking me senseless. Heat rushes through me as my imagination fills with me and Ace somewhere alone. He's feasting on my drenched pussy as I moan his name over and over. His big hands grip my hips tight, holding me still until he's devoured me completely.

"Hey. Dottie!" Ace says.

"Yes. Sorry. I was off in thought." I wipe my lips with the back of my hand and gulp as I notice the sweat on his muscular biceps. God, I want to know how good he must taste. I blink rapidly and focus on the reality before me. Ace is my handyman, not my lover.

"Where'd you go?" Ace stands and comes toward me. He holds the door frame with his hand placed above my head.

I glance up and into his gorgeous eyes. I trail my tongue over my lips as my breathing intensifies. He's so close to me. Too close. I inhale his rough, sweaty scent. The heat radiating from him makes my clit throb. I close my eyes and imagine him pulling me to him, pressing his strong body against me.

"Hey." Ace touches my shoulder, squeezing it gently. "Are you okay?"

I draw in a quick breath, then let it out to hide a wish for him to take me right here, right now.

"Um… Oh, yes. I'm good, Ace. Are you finished fixing

the sink?" I ask to focus on something other than my fantasies about him.

"It's okay if you're not okay, Dottie. I'll do anything for you." He leans down, his lips brush my ear as he whispers, "Anything at all." His hand slides down my arm to my hand. He takes it in his. Bringing it to his cheek, he presses his face into my palm. His skin is amazingly soft.

I sigh, tilting my head. When our eyes meet, his piercing gaze of desire and need fill me with heat. We're alone. No one would know.

His warm breath grazes my cheek, then my lips.

I jerk back and say, "I can't. Ace. I'm sorry. You don't understand. I want to, but I can't." I turn and rush down the stairs.

When Ace comes into the kitchen, I'm waiting for him with my phone in my hand ready to pay him through Venmo.

"How much?" I ask without meeting his gaze.

"Dottie, I'm sorry. That won't happen again. I care about you." He reaches for me, but I step back.

I can't allow this beautiful man to get hurt by wanting me. My husband hates me, and he'll never allow me a moment of peace. Ace deserves better than me. I'm married and not available.

"How much for the repair, Ace?" I ask again.

"Don't worry about this one, honey. Please keep my number in a safe place. I'll do whatever you need me to, Dottie. I promise." He brushes my arm gently, then turns and leaves through the garage.

"**D**ottie," Ivan bellows as I make my way downstairs. Our kids have left for school already, so my husband's real self comes out in full force. I brace for whatever he has for me.

"Yes, dear. I'm right here. No need to yell," I say softly as I enter the kitchen.

"What the hell is this?" He shoves the paperwork from all the recent repairs Ace has left invoices for against my chest when I get close enough to him.

I flinch. Taking the paper, I wince and rub my sore chest. Glancing at them, my mouth runs dry. "Oh, a few things broke while you were gone," I try to say, my pulse thundering in my skull. I didn't do anything with Ace, but is Ivan upset just because I had another man in the house? "I had everything repaired," I babble. "I tried to call you, but you never answered, or returned my calls. So, I just took care of having it all fixed." I stand frozen, waiting for what he'll do. Defending myself only makes it worse.

Lurching forward, he grabs my arm, his fingers digging painfully into my flesh. When I catch his glare, I shiver. His mean teeth-clenched grin terrifies me, but I don't dare try to get free. I know it's useless to try.

Ivan stands at six-foot-five and is two-hundred-twenty pounds of pure muscle. He works out daily and eats clean. I'm only five-foot-three and one-hundred-twenty pounds. After each baby, I had to drop the weight as fast as possible. Ivan has an image we both must uphold. A mere month after my three pregnancies, he hired a personal trainer to come to the house and forced me to get back to my pre-baby body. I suffered a uterine rupture with our second baby, but he did not care.

"Jesus Christ. A thousand dollars for these minor repairs? Fuck, that's robbery, Dottie. Did you even try to negotiate it down?" His grip tightens hard enough to bruise, but I breathe out in relief.

He complains about money all the time. There's no need to; we have plenty. A thousand dollars is nothing. His job as the top defense lawyer in South Beach, Florida, pays very well. And if it's just this that has made him mad, I can soothe him.

Placing a hand on his chest, I shake my head. "No, Ivan, I didn't. I'm sorry I'm stupid. But I did try to let you know in advance. Unfortunately, we needed the repairs done as soon as possible. I'm sorry."

Silence fills the room as Ivan releases me and reads all of the paperwork. He glances at me, then goes back to reading. Once finished, he asks, "Were you alone with him?"

A chill rushes through me. My heart slows as an ache pierces it. "No," I say, crossing my arms, instinctively trying to defend my body. "I just let him in to do the work, but I didn't stay."

"So you left him in the house alone? Jesus! I bet he robbed us!"

I flinch. "Ace wouldn't –"

"You're on a first-name basis with him then?" he roars, standing and moving toward me.

I stumble back.

"You've been fucking him in my own house, haven't you?" He grabs me.

"No! Ivan. I swear I –"

But he doesn't listen. He never listens.

A few years back, I tried to leave. Liam, the security guard who worked for the Beau Monde Estates property management company, planned to help get me and my children away from Ivan.

One day, when I came home from SILK, the spa Ivan allowed me to go to every so often, Liam stopped me at the front entrance gate. I'd only had my hair done that day, and wore a long-sleeved blouse because of several bruises on my body that I didn't want anyone at SILK to see. But Liam had seen the bruise on my wrist when I drove up to the guardhouse where he sits for his eight-hour shift. My hands were on the steering wheel which tugged up my long-sleeved blouse, revealing the bruises.

Despite me saying no several times, Liam insisted he help me and my children escape from Ivan. He told me his plan to have me get my kids from school early and tell them I was taking them to a program at the local library. All my kids love to read, so it made sense to use the library as a cover.

On the day we'd planned to escape, I went out to pick up my children, Liam wasn't at his post. He said he'd be in the guard house that morning. Instantly, worry and chills filled my body. The hairs on the back of my neck stood up. A darkness engulfed me when a few minutes later as I drove toward the school, I heard on the radio that a man was found in one of the canals that run behind the community. They reported the man was near death and was transported to May's hospital.

I nearly drove my car into a cement light pole, but hit the brakes just in time. I sat in my car, tears filled my eyes. I wasn't sure if the man was Liam, but the ache inside me made me think it was him.

Once I got myself calmed down, I returned home and unpacked all of the small bags I'd packed for me and my children. I did my best to act normal when my kids got home from school, and when Ivan returned from his business trip.

Dinner was ready and the table was set as usual, but Ivan came into the kitchen and grabbed me hard by my arm. His hot breath hissed against my skin when he told me he'd taken care of my friend. He warned me to never try to leave him and take his children from him. He'd kill me and anyone who'd try to help me.

When our kids were in bed, he drug me to the garage and taught me a lesson on how to be *his* wife. My body ached for weeks afterwards. The bruises on my torso took longer to heal. But the damage to me mentally never healed. My fears of Ivan stayed with me.

Ivan was questioned by the police several times, and each time he said he didn't know who Liam was. Ivan was a great liar. He'd lie to his own parents if it meant he'd be able to live as he pleased.

Eventually, Ivan was arrested for Liam's death. I didn't know that Liam had died until Ivan was formally charged. I hadn't dared to check up on Liam while he was in the hospital as I was sure Ivan had people watching me and my phone was bugged.

Unfortunately for me, Ivan's case was dismissed. One of his partner's managed to get him off on a technicality. It seemed he and his lawyer friends were very good at getting the guilty off scot-free.

After all that mess was over, I've been terrified to even think of leaving Ivan. I can't leave my kids behind to save myself from my husband's abuse. I do my best to be his perfect wife with everything in its place. Dinner ready on time. His clothes washed, ironed, folded, and put away exactly as he showed me he wants them to be.

But, I'm not perfect and I pay the price for that when Ivan finds something wrong. He teaches me my lesson for messing up even the tiniest of things. Those lessons leave bruises to remind me how to be Ivan's perfect wife.

The moment I first saw her, I saw the sadness in her eyes. I see it every time I come to her house to repair whatever she asks me to. I see the emptiness. The desperation to be free. I long to set Dottie free from the bondage of her marriage to the coldest man I've ever met, Ivan Andreev III Esq. A woman should be treasured and treated like a queen. Dottie would be my queen if I ever got that chance.

I don't care if I don't know how to fix whatever Dottie needs fixed. I'll Google it and learn. Anything to help her and see her. She's the most beautiful older woman I've ever met. She deserves the best, and I plan to give it to her. I just need to find a way to release her from this unhappy life she leads.

My phone pings with the special sound I assigned to her.

Dottie: Are you busy today?

Me: No. What do you need, Dottie?

Dottie: My dishwasher is dinging. I tried to reset it, but it won't stop dinging.

Me: I'll be right over.

Dottie: Thank you, Ace.

Me: You're welcome. Anything for you.

Grabbing my work bag and tool belt from the garage, I quickly make my way to Dottie's. Even in her texts, I know she needs me for more than fixing the dishwasher.

"Thank you so much, Ace, for coming on short notice," Dottie says as she steps aside to let me enter her home. "I don't know what I'd do without you." She lays her soft hand on my forearm.

I go to pat her hand and notice a bruise on the top of it. This is the first time I've seen marks on Dottie. I know her husband hurts her mentally. But I didn't know he abuses her physically. Stopping myself from touching her hand, I raise my eyes. First up her long-sleeved shirt. *She always wears long sleeves*... Then to her eyes.

She quickly removes her hand from me, shifting her gaze away. "The dishwasher," she says. "Please."

Turning away from me, she leads me into the kitchen, even though I know my way around the Andreev residence like it's my own home.

"Is he home?" I ask as I follow her. He never is, but I want to be sure he won't interrupt us today. I've waited too long to save Dottie, and that's guilt I'll now have to live with forever. But if he's putting hands on her, I'm getting her away today.

Skittishly, she shakes her head.

As we enter the kitchen, I grab her non-bruised hand and tug her to face me. A faint mark peeking out of her shirt on her chest grabs my attention. I'd not seen it when I first got here, being distracted by the bruise on her hand. My neck heats as I think of how she got that mark.

"How are you, Dottie? Like, really. Honestly." I squeeze her hand gently.

Shaking her head, she tries to pull her blouse over the mark on her chest. "It's nothing," she whispers. "I'm fine."

"No, you're not. Sit here and tell me the truth." I walk her to the breakfast nook table and pull out a chair for her. I slide another one close to her and sit beside her. "Now, Dottie. Tell me where you got that bruise on your hand and the mark on your chest. I'm not leaving until you tell me who did that to you." I place two fingers under her chin and turn her head toward me. Tears stream down her soft, pale skin.

"Ace, I... It's... No." She tries to stand. I gently, but firmly hold her so she can't.

"Dottie. I'll protect you. But I need to know the truth. We'll find a way to help you and your children. I promise." Tenderly squeezing her hand, I tug lightly to get her to look at me.

"You can't help me. He'll kill you, Ace. He will. He has connections to awful people. It's too dangerous. I'll be fine." Freeing herself from me, she stands, then walks to the other side of the kitchen. Putting distance between us.

Rising from the chair, I follow her and grasp her dainty shoulders. I embrace her as she collapses against me. She shivers in my arms. Sobbing, she comes completely unraveled.

She whispers, "I wish he were dead."

Wanting to help Dottie escape her abusive marriage, I dig deep into her husband, Ivan Andreev, III. Esq. There must be something I can find to hold over him and get Dottie her freedom.

I reach out to a couple of friends with connections in the DA's office who owe me favors. Most of the time they play on the level, but Ivan's sleazy reputation helps my friends to be willing to give me the evidence that was thrown out of the bench trial by the crooked judge hearing Ivan's case. I fucking hate these mother fuckers with all this money. They believe they can do whatever the hell they want and the rest of us have to live by the rule of law.

Yeah, fuck that shit. With this evidence I have on Ivan, I could ruin him, but I know he'll make Dottie pay for it if I expose him publicly. So I stop by Defense Dynasty. The young woman at the front desk asks my name and who I am there to see.

"Ivan Andreev. I don't have an appointment, but I need to see him now." I stand tall with the manila envelope tucked under my arm.

"Mr. Andreev only sees clients with appointments. Your name is?" she asks.

"Ace. Just Ace. Let Ivan know I'm here and it's urgent that we speak now," I demand.

"Mr. Ace. I'm sorry, but Mr. Andreev—"

"I. Don't. Care. Get him on the damn phone and tell him I'm on my way up." I wave her off and step toward the elevators to my right. When a security guard stops me at the elevators, I say, "You don't want to get fired, so I'd let me get on the elevator. I have extremely important information for Ivan."

The guard looks me up and down, then a voice comes across his walkie-talkie telling him to let me pass. He nods and moves out of my way.

On the sixth floor, the elevator doors slide open. I step out and walk toward the black desk that sits in front of two enormous double white marble doors. Another attractive, young woman stands and meets me in front of her desk.

"Mr. Andreev is waiting for you, Mr. Ace." She leads me to the double doors, then swings one open. "Mr. Ace, sir," she says to Ivan, who's seated behind a mahogany desk. Floor to ceiling windows line the back wall of his office facing the east. The Atlantic Ocean is in the distance.

"Ace. What has Dottie asked of you that made you demand to see me?" Ivan asks, tapping a pen against his chin.

"Dottie has no idea that I'm here. This is between you and me, Ivan." I stand tall and hold the manila envelope out in front of me.

Ivan takes the envelope and opens it. His face darkens as he reads the damning evidence that can put him in jail or even get him the death penalty if it were to come out.

I stand with my arms crossed, waiting for him to react.

He rises from his leather chair and comes out from behind

the desk. He slaps my arms with the envelope, then steps closer, leaning into me. "Whatever the fuck you think this is. It's not. I'm capable of making Dottie and you disappear and no one will ever find either of you. Is that what you want?" he hisses. His face tightens as redness creeps up his neck. His eyes narrow as he waits for me to speak.

I hold my place and push him back a step. "You touch one hair on Dottie again and you'll disappear. I fucking swear this envelope will be made public if she even has a tiny scratch on her anywhere. I know you think you own her, but you don't. She deserves better than shit like you."

Ivan yanks my arm hard. "You punk. I'll fucking kill you!" he threatens, baring his teeth at me.

I don't move. I stand strong and push him hard again. The back of his thighs hit his desk with a thud.

"The fuck, you will. I've left instructions that if I can't be reached by those who know me, this evidence goes public. I've also made arrangements for Dottie and *her* children to be cared for in your absence."

"You're fucking crazy if you think you can take my family from me. I'm calling security." Ivan reaches to his left and lifts the desk phone from its cradle.

"Go ahead. The envelope gets released immediately unless you agree to leave and go back to Belarus. And never contact Dottie again. I don't care what excuse you use to tell your partners and clients, but make it a convincing one."

Ivan lurches and grabs the envelope from me, tearing it in half. His face is completely red with anger. He huffs heavily as he throws the torn envelope at me.

"It wasn't the only copy, in case you thought I was that stupid. I may be just a handyman, but I have friends in high places too. And my friends don't take bribes that can get them thrown in jail. Unlike you, Ivan. I live a clean, honest life. I'm good to people. I treat everyone the same. But…" I pause and drag my hand through my hair. "Fuckers like you. Abusers, liars, killers, and real pieces of shit. You deserve the worst. And I intend to see you get what you deserve."

"You're not man enough to do any of this," Ivan says, his brow furrows as he paces his office.

"Try me, then. I promise you, you'll be arrested before I leave this building." I glance at my phone. A text from one of my friends asking if he needs to send the information to the proper authorities.

I hide my friend's name and show Ivan the text.

> Boss, do I need to pass on the evidence to our trusted contact?

"Fuck," Ivan hisses. He stomps back to his desk and shoves his chair against it. "Fuck, fuck, fuck." He splays his hands on his desk and says through clenched teeth, "Fine. I'll leave. I'll be in Belarus by midnight."

Not believing him, I say, "You're going to have to prove it to me. I know this law firm has a private jet, so call it up and get it ready for you. I'll wait." I sit in the large leather chair opposite Ivan's desk chair.

He picks up his cell phone from the desk and taps on the screen. He says into the phone, "Mick, I need the jet ready now to go to Belarus. Family emergency." A brief silence while whoever Mick is talks to Ivan. "Don't worry about it. I'll talk to them. I need it more. They can fly commercial. Just do it." He ends the call and turns to me. "Convinced yet?' he asks.

"No. I'll follow you to the airport and watch you board the jet and take off. I'll wait until I feel it's safe enough to go and get Dottie. She'll take care of her children." I push the chair back and stand. "Never, ever try to contact her or try to find her. I'll take care of her forever. And I'll take care of her children. You don't need to worry about them." I walk toward the door and wait for Ivan to leave first. I follow him out of the building and all the way to the small private airport.

Waiting in the private jet hangars, I nod as he boards the Defense Dynasty's private jet. Once it's in the air and I'm sure on its way to Belarus, I get in my truck and go to Dottie.

Dottie

❧

"Ace. What's going on? What's wrong?" I ask as he rushes into my house when I answer the door.

"I need you to pack for you and your kids. Just the necessities for now. We can come back for more when I'm sure it's safe." He paces the entryway, beads of sweat are on his forehead.

"Ace, why?" I ask.

"Dottie, please. It's not safe here right now. I'm taking you and your children to a safe house for a few days. I'll fill you in when we get there. Please go pack. And quickly." He nudges me gently toward the grand staircase.

I convince my kids to pack a small bag with just their necessities and promise we will be back for the rest. I tell them we're going on an adventure for a few days. When they ask about Ivan, I tell them that he's on an important business trip and we'll see him when he returns. They accept everything I tell them and pack as I ask of them.

"Ace, where are we going?" I ask after my kids are in the SUV and buckled in.

"It's a safe house far enough away from here to keep you

and your children from harm." He leans closer and whispers into my ear, "I took care of Ivan."

I step back, my mouth agape. "Is he…" I let my words trail off.

"He's fine. He's on his way to Belarus and won't be back for a while. I need you and the kids to stay away from here until I'm sure he understands everything I told him. And he understands that I'm going to take care of you forever."

"Ace." I hug him tightly, tears beginning to fall down my cheek. "Thank you."

"Anything for you, Dottie. I love you." Ace holds me for a few more seconds then he releases me and says, "We need to get on the road, honey."

When we arrive at the safe house, my children and I unpack our bags in our respective rooms. Ace knocks softly on my bedroom door.

"Hey, all settled?" he asks and sits on the end of the bed.

"I think so. Will you tell me how you got Ivan to agree to all of this?" I ask, sitting next to him.

"Dottie, your husband isn't the only one with connections. But my connections are good, law-abiding friends. He's not ever going to bother you. I promise. Or he'll go to jail and die there."

"Ace, what do you have on him?" I ask and swallow hard. Fear creeps up my spine as I know how ruthless Ivan can be. I know he must have fought Ace before giving in.

"You don't need to worry about that. I've got all my bases covered. My friends have their instructions. If anything happens to you, your children, or me, Ivan will go to jail." Ace takes my hands in his. He lifts them to his lips and kisses my knuckles. "It's over, Dottie. You're free. I have a lawyer friend coming tomorrow to help you file for divorce."

I shake my head, "He won't sign the papers. He won't, Ace. I know my husband."

"Honey, you need to trust me. What I have on Ivan… well he won't refuse to do anything I tell him to." He tugs on my hands and I tilt my head. "I swear," he promises, then kisses me tenderly.

I want to let go and trust Ace with all my heart, but a small pinch tells me to be cautious.

Dottie

After signing the divorce papers, I was shocked to receive a final decree within a few weeks. Ace came through for me. His promises held up. I still don't know what he has on my now ex-husband, Ivan Andreev, but I don't care anymore. I'm free and can live free with Ace.

I told my children as much as I felt they could handle. I hope one day I can tell them the entire truth about why their parents' marriage failed. They must understand that it was never their fault. Their father is a difficult man. He's a flawed human, but I know he loves our children.

They are allowed to visit with him every other weekend, supervised for now. When they return they tell me all about their time with Ivan. How much he spoils them with new clothes and takes them to the amusement parks.

We moved in with Ace after my divorce was final. His house is big enough for each of my kids to have their own rooms.

I'm free to be me again. Free to be with a man who adores me. Who worships me. Who loves my children as his own. The man who loves me as much as I love him.

Ace sweeps me from my feet as soon as I open the door to greet him when he comes home from work. His mouth smashes to mine before I can utter a sound. His tongue glides along my lips, then pushes into my mouth. This is our weekend alone, so I don't stop Ace's passionate kisses.

He tastes so fucking amazing. His lips are soft. His mustache tickles my face as he holds the nape of my neck with one hand.

I slide down his body, standing on my feet again. Wrapping my arms around his perfect body, I embrace him tightly.

His arms tighten around me as we kiss deeply for several minutes in the foyer of what is now our home. When we finally pull apart, he cups my cheeks with his large hands, caressing them with his thumbs. The passion and desire in his hazel eyes penetrates me to my heart.

I grip his forearms, staring wantonly at him.

His hands engulf my shoulders as his eyes trail down my body. When his gaze comes back to mine, he says, "God, you're stunning. I want you, Dottie. I've wanted you since the first day I saw you. Baby, you deserve to be happy, loved, and fulfilled completely." Ace leans down, kissing me again.

My heart pounds fiercely. My body quivers with excitement, knowing he wants me as I want him. Wrapping my arms around him again, I slide my hands under his shirt and up his back. I pull him tighter to me, feeling his hard cock against my stomach. I tilt my head as a grin tugs at my lips. Fuck, how I want this man.

"I want you too, Ace. I always have," I say, sliding my hands down his back.

He takes my hand in his and leads me down the hall to our bedroom.

Standing by our bed, I begin to untie the sash on my black silk robe so he can see the red negligee I put on for him.

He stops me, saying, "Let me take care of you, Dottie. Like you deserve, love." He stands in front of me, ripping off his T-shirt before beginning to undress me.

He takes his time with me, like I'm a delicate flower about to bloom. He hooks his index fingers under each of the lacy straps of my negligee, tugging them down my arm.

My breasts fall free once the lacy fabric drops to my waist when I sit on the end of the bed.

"My god, you're perfect," Ace says as he leans down. Placing his soft hands on my knees, he kisses my left breast. His tongue licks my stiff nipple, sending sensual pulses through me.

I thread my fingers through his thick curly hair. My head falls back as he continues sucking on one breast while kneading the other. I place my hands behind me to brace myself. Ace's tongue drives me wild for him. My pussy throbs and aches for his attention.

He trails his mouth down my body, kissing my navel, then gently tugging on the negligee around my waist. I lift my ass enough for him to slide it from me. With his hands on my thighs, he spreads me wide.

"Ace," I purr as he kisses my clit, then slides his tongue along my drenched pussy. "Oh my god," I moan.

He lifts my legs onto his broad shoulders, then kisses my pussy tenderly before completely devouring me. He licks me. Kisses me. Sucks me.

My arousal climbs quickly as I try to pinch my legs against his head.

He stops me by placing his big hands on my inner thighs. He eats me like I'm his most treasured delicacy that he's not had in forever.

I shatter from sexual pleasures I've never felt before. I scream, "Ace, dear lord. Baby, oh, Ace! Ace!" I grab the sheets, pulling them hard.

He continues his full ravaging of my pussy, making my orgasms climb to the highest of highs. To new levels of majestic euphoria, where my body explodes with joy. They leave me wanting more and more of Ace.

Grabbing his arm as he reaches for my breast, I can't help but buck against his mouth. "God. Oh, my god, baby. Yes! Yes! Yes!" I jolt upright, then fall back onto the bed, breathless.

"Mmm," Ace purrs against my clit. He lifts himself from his position between my legs and crawls onto me. Leaning down, he kisses me tenderly.

"Oh, baby," I pant as his long, hard cock plunges inside me. I arch my back, pressing into him as he moves his hips slowly.

"I want to make love to you, Dottie. Slow, sweet love." Ace kisses me deeply as he carefully slides his arms under and around me. His hips continue a slow rhythm, up and down as his cock fucks me beautifully.

I kiss him back with all the love I have hidden from him since we met. I whisper, "I love you, Ace. I always have." My hands cup his scruffy face.

His eyes meet mine, and a satisfying grin tugs at his lips. He kisses me again and again while we make love. He feels amazing.

"I love you too, Dottie." Ace's embrace tightens as his body stiffens when he comes. "God, how I love you." He props himself up with his elbows on either side of my head and smiles wide. "I don't want to spend another minute without you."

"There's still a lot to figure out, Ace."

"Don't worry about a thing. Together, we can conquer anything. Anything at all, baby."

Epilogue

ACE

"**D**ottie!" I call out when I enter our house.

"I'm in the kitchen," she says.

I grab her around her waist and spin her from her feet.

"Oh my goodness, Ace. What's that for?" she asks after I set her back down.

"Watch," I say and grab the remote, turning on the TV hanging above the bar.

I stand next to Dottie with my arm around her shoulder. I squeeze it gently, then lean down and kiss her soft lips.

The newscaster announces, "Top story tonight. There's been an arrest pertaining to the young man who was found murdered several years ago. Ivan Andreev, III. Esquire, has been taken into custody and charged with Liam Peterson's murder. Yes, Mr. Andreev had been set free the last time he was on trial for the same murder, but in that case the judge dismissed the case on a technicality…"

"Oh my god!" Dottie screams. "Ace, is this true? Ivan's been arrested and charged. He's really going to prison this time. He's really going to have to pay for murdering Liam. Oh my god!" she rattles off, her eyes are the size of saucers.

"Yes, honey. It's all true. I decided he needed to pay for his crime. I had my friends hand over all the evidence we had on Ivan. It's too much evidence for him to skate free this time. He's going away for a long time, maybe forever." I embrace her and kiss the top of her head.

Her arms wrap around me and squeeze me tightly. "I can't believe it." She begins to cry, her body jerks with her sobs.

"What's wrong, sweetheart?" I ask as I hold her against my chest.

"Will you help me tell my children? I don't think I can do that alone. They're going to need our love and support."

"Of course, honey. I'll do anything for you."

She tilts her head and pushes her body up on her tip-toes. Our lips meet in a tender kiss. When our kiss ends, she says, "I love you, Ace."

"I love you too, Dottie. Forever."

Thank You

To my husband, Randy, for his never-ending love and support throughout this entire process.

My friends and family for their love and support.

Miranda.
Thank you for your guidance since the beginning of my indie publishing journey.
I wouldn't be where I am without you.
You're the best!

Tori.
Thank you for all the beautiful covers and all the amazing graphics you've created for me.

My wonderful readers.
Thank you for taking a chance on me and making this dream possible.

Books By KC Savage

Love, Emma Series:

The Encounter

The Choice

The Decision

Escape To Wonderland:

The Club Wonderland Series

Forbidden Spice

3000 Miles

The Silent Sins Duet:

A Dual Lie

A Secret Lie

Beau Monde Estates:

Blown

Drenched

Plugged

Screwed

Pin Me

About KC Savage

KC lives in Florida with her husband.

She loves to write and read forbidden, taboo, cheating romances.
When she's not busy creating her next sizzling story, KC spends her free time with her husband and family.
Some of her favorite places are Las Vegas, NYC, and the beach watching the sunsets.

🌟 Sign up to KC's monthly newsletter here: 🌟
https://dashboard.mailerlite.com/forms/526938/ 111277544350680076/share

Links and places to follow to keep up with KC:

www.kcsavageauthor.com

https://allmylinks.com/kcsavage

www.ingramcontent.com/pod-product-compliance
Lightning Source LLC
Chambersburg PA
CBHW071943190726
48293CB00004B/1319